W9-CKC-286

Boxer and Beauty
A Tale of Two Cart-horses

Boxer and Beauty
A Tale of Two Cart-horses

Alfred Ollivant

ASHFORD
Southampton

First published in 1924 by William Heinemann Ltd

This edition published in 1989 by Ashford, 1 Church Road,
Shedfield, Hampshire SO3 2HW

Although every effort has been made we have been unable
to trace the copyright owner for this title. We would
therefore welcome any information which would enable us
to do so.

All rights reserved. Except for use in review, no part of this
book may be reproduced or utilised in any form or by any
means electronic or mechanical, including photocopying,
recording or by any information storage and retrieval
system, without permission from the publisher.

British Library Cataloguing in Publication Data

Ollivant, Alfred
  Boxer and Beauty: a tale of two cart-horses –
  (Ashford animal classics)
  I. Title
  823′.8[F]

  ISBN 1–85253–164–9

Phototypeset by Input Typesetting Ltd, London
Printed by Hartnolls Limited, Bodmin, Cornwall, England

Contents

Foreword

In the years immediately following the 1914–18 war, the "war to end all wars", the idea became firmly rooted in the minds of those who had survived the blood-letting that before 1914 there had been a golden age of certainty and success, an Elysian climax to the striving of their Victorian forebears. It was in this climate that Alfred Ollivant, author of the now better remembered *Bob, Son of Battle*, conceived of Gallops farm in the East Riding of Yorkshire, a seemingly impregnable redoubt against a gathering storm of change. Here the Lord family, yeoman farmers for over 150 years, cleaved to their 800 acres, taking as their creed the more utilitarian values of the Victorian era — duty, hard work, thrift, self-sacrifice — and reinforcing their faith with an almost impenetrable refrain in the local dialect, "Gallops got to goo on soom gait". No "scrimshanking" was allowed. "You did what you were paid to do, full measure and perhaps a little over, or you went."

In reality, even before the "cloud-burst of blood" had broken over Europe, the harmony and stability of rural life had been undermined by the agricultural depression of the 1870s, the increased use of labour-saving machinery and the defection of farm-workers from the villages to the higher wages of the towns. Gallops, however, appears to be untouched by these changing circumstances, its more obvious nemesis being the Great War which drains the farm of men, horses, peace and harmony. In fact the seeds of dissent and disorder had been sown before the beginning of the war in the conflict between Old William, "Lord Gord" himself, who can see nothing beyond the material prosperity of Gallops, and "Young Will" Lord, the head-horseman, whose love for the two cart-horses, Boxer and Beauty, surpasses even his familial loyalty to the farm.

Will's affections, "deep and quiet as an inland sea", are sadly out of place in a world dominated by profit and stultifying dogma, as out of place as his other — requisitioned — horses are pulling artillery on the Somme. His pleasure lies in training and working the mighty Boxer and the besotted Beauty, harnessing their combined strength and diverse temperaments to make, with him, a team that can draw life and wealth from the land. He is mortified at the very thought of either of his two "bright bays" being sold into the towns, those "obscene ogres" always lurking on the borders of this rural idyll.

Will's is a simple vision of man and beast in harmony. In a world in flux it is all that he has to hold on to, even as Old William has only the farm, but in an age darkened by the complexity and contrivance of man's affairs, it is not enough. Will remains true to his beloved Boxer, and Boxer will bear no other master, but the almost primal bond between them is betrayed by a family and a world divided against itself.

CHAPTER ONE

Gallops

Boxer and Beauty were bred on Gallops Farm in the East Riding. Gallops was a big farm for England; some eight hundred acres, lime-stone in the main, heavily-treed, well-watered, with big dykes between the fields, and strong hedges: ideal land for raising stock.

And a stock-farm Gallops was, though some half of it was given up to the plough. There were twenty men or more on it all the year round — horse-men, as they call the carters in the North, cow-men, shepherds, labourers, lads; and a wench or two — besides Martha Lord.

The Lords of Gallops were almost as well-known in that country as the Cavendishes or the Howards. Simple farmers, who never pretended to be anything more, they were of the old yeomen-race, once the back-bone of

1

England, to-day almost extinct. They had owned the farm and known no overman since before the Industrial Revolution. *Gallops got to goo on soom gait*, was the motto on which five generations had been brought up, and the motive behind all the drive and sweat and hard-bargaining that had kept the farm in the family for a century and a half.

And Gallops looked as if it would remain in possession of the Lords a long while yet: for Gallops meant Old William, who had been known familiarly to his hands, to Birkby Whin, and even to remote Barnston, as Lord Gord ever since he succeeded his father. He had earned his name too. A masterful man, covetous, severe, but just, he dominated the farm by sheer force of personality. There was never any doubt that Gallops would go on so long as Old William did; and there was very little doubt that it would go on after him: for he had four sons, the fruit of his sour-faced money-making missus, who had brought forth and multiplied against the grain, it seemed, in order that the family passion, which had entered into her blood and obsessed her too, might be fulfilled. Daughters Martha Lord had none; nor would you have expected it.

George was the eldest of the four boys, his father's prop, his mother's pride. You had only to look at him to know that while George lived

Gallops would be safe. A short thick man, the antithesis of his voluminous father, stocky, with a bruiser's neck, and a close-cropped small black head, there was pugnacity in every inch of him. He went about the farm at his swift stumpy walk that was almost a run, his little brown eyes everywhere, barking an order here, shooting a podgy authoritative fist there, nothing escaping him.

No wonder his mother who admired little, admired him: George was that strong and bossy, same as his dad. His qualities, indeed, were so like his father's that Old William might well have been jealous. But he was not. With all his faults there was a certain bigness about the old man, that corresponded to his physical bulk, and accounted perhaps for the weight of his authority. If he was greedy he could be generous too. And when his eye fell on George his heart felt good within him. He saw in his son not the heir who would some day supplant him but the captain who would hold the fort against all comers long after he was gone. Yes; Gallops was safe enough sure for at least another generation, and beyond, aye, beyond. It was impossible to believe that George with his thick legs and sturdy bull-neck that burnt a deep-red under the summer sun could ever die.

George was foreman of Gallops before he

was twenty, and had won his place too. On the farm everything gave way to efficiency, even primogeniture. Gallops came first. If you could not serve Gallops at the top, even though your name was Lord, then you made room for a Lord who could, and took yourself a lower place suited exactly to your capacity, or, better still, took yourself out of it and beyond seas where there might be room for the likes of you. In the history of the Lords this thing had happened.

George was respected by the hands if he was not liked. That is to say although he was a bit of a bully like his father, he dealt out a rough and ready justice. Under George there was no scrimshanking. You did what you were paid to do, full measure and perhaps a little over, or you went.

Often Old William gave thanks secretly that Young Will came second. Young Will was nobody's son, as his mother was fond of telling the lanky youth: a bit of a dreamer, but a worker too, as everybody at Gallops had to be, with a certain marked talent of his own.

"Will's a genius with horses, Mr. Lord," Mr. Thorp, the vicar of Birkby Whin, said to Old William at the Barnston Shire-horse Show, as they stood together at the ringside and watched the lad, only just left school, leading by a vast mare, her woolly-tailed foal at foot.

"He's not such a fool at *that* job, I will allow," Old William mumbled.

"Will's a dear," piped little Esther Thorp, clutching her father's hand. "I love him."

"You love the foal, dearie," said Old William, lifting the child up. "There! he's won t' prize. They're puttin the red riband on him. Esmeralda's foal he is. Bounce, I think Will calls him — because he's that bouncy."

"I love the foal too," said grave little Esther.

She loved Will partly for his own sake, but much more because of his love of horses, a passion that she shared in full.

Once a noble lady, taking the child round an old garden fragrant with verbenas, stocks, carnations, had asked her what smell she liked best.

Esther had answered with characteristic solemnity in a voice already deep,

"Hot horse."

CHAPTER TWO

The Head-horseman

Stock-men, as every farmer knows, are born not made. That intimate communion which prevails between some men and animals, based on sympathy, and giving the power that is established on the sure rock of understanding, seems to run in the main in families, and be handed down from father to son not by precept but mysteriously in the blood. You have it; or you haven't. If you haven't you will never acquire it. And you have a better chance of having it if your father had it before you. That is all there is to say.

"Yo can learn em the land," Old William would say. "But God made the stock-man."

And if God made the stock-man He seems to have evolved him, as He evolved all else, by degrees, after endless experiment and even failure. And first He made the cow-man, and then the shepherd, and last, the crowning creation in this particular type, the horse-man.

A man may be firstrate with cattle — the rearing of calves, the handling of fratchy cows, the fattening of bullocks, the humouring of bulls; clever with sheep; and yet not particular with horses — or the other way about.

Young Will was like that. Not out of the ordinary with other stock, with horses he was a miracle-man.

"Will's got t' way wi em," Old William, reluctantly compelled to admire, said to his shrewish wife.

"Just as well," Martha replied. "He's good for nowt beside."

All the heart the hard woman had to give had long ago been lavished on George and George's father. Indeed she was the not uncommon type of woman who bows her neck meekly and with joy to the domineer while herself riding rough-shod over the gentle man.

Her husband had found out all that in the early days of marriage, as shrewd husbands do.

"Yo got to ride Mart," he confided to his father. "Then she answers to it."

"They mostly doos," replied the Lord of that day with the shrewd natural sagacity that had kept him and his on top for over a century.

"Coax-y don't work wi Mart," added the

7

young husband, shaking the knowing head of the newly-married man who was discovering for himself afresh the things each successive generation of husbands discover. "It's whip she do adore."

Young Will was no tyrant and his mother despised him accordingly. He was a Christian who never went to church; and his mother, who did go, was a Pagan, and a primitive one at that.

Born in another station in life, with solitude and leisure in which to brood, Will might have been a poet. But at Gallops there was no time for roaming in the fields, and absorbing beauty. The fields were there to be cleaned, disciplined, and made fruitful. It was all stir-about. You had to get on wi it or goo.

Not that Young Will was a scholar or wished to be. He had not done well at his books either in the village-school at Birkby Whin or during the term or two he passed at the grammar-school in Barnston. In fact he hadn't done as well as George, the Philistine, who had proved himself as forceful and tenacious in the school-room as he had done on the farm. But Will read. Even when he was pretty nigh man-grown he never entirely conquered that habit. That was one of the counts his mother had against him. He read when he should have been doing, or resting from doing — the two processes natural to man.

When she caught him at it she banged about and shewed genuine resentment.

"Can't yo find somethin better'n that to do then?" she would snap. "Settin lazin there over book-trash! Better by far get on wi it." And that was always the cry.

Old William, a man of peace so long as Gallops went on, shewed a certain sympathy with the lad and would come to his rescue.

"Leave t' lad a-be, Mother," he would mutter. "There's all sorts. Books winna hurt him so long as they doesna keep him from his work."

And they never did that. Will had his place like his brother George, and was worth it. If he had not been he would never have held it. On the farm every worker was a cog in the great machine which ground out its day's work to the monotonous refrain — *Gallops got to goo on soom gait*.

Will had won his place on the farm very simply in the beginning. When the second stable-lad enlisted suddenly, Young Will deserted school without authority or notice. His father, going the rounds, found him leading a team when the bottoms were being ploughed in Wey Pastures, and keeping the leader's nose well into the hedge as if born to the job.

9

"I thought yo was at school, Will," he grunted.

"I'm horse-man's mate to Joe there," the lad replied briefly.

Old William turned inquiringly to the second horse-man at the handle of the plough.

"He's a help to Oi, Will be," that worthy replied, drawing a leathern sleeve elaborately across his nose.

Lord Gord accepted the *fait accompli* philosophically. Young Will's passion was well-known, and his powers could be used for the glory of Gallops.

Gradually the lad worked his way up. He became head stable-lad, horse-man in time, and finally head horse-man of Gallops. There he stayed, his ambition satisfied. Earth had nothing more to offer him.

Old William said nothing. Soon he left the whole of the horse-management on the farm to his second son. Will bought for him, sold for him, selected the sires, saw to the mating, handled the foals, broke the young stuff himself. Old William knew very well that Young Will was the best horse-master in the district, and as a vet. second only to himself. And he was quite content to leave it at that.

George too let Will alone. That was the best of George — once he had satisfied himself that you knew your job and did it he never interfered with you. And there was no question that Will knew his job.

George did not understand his younger brother and did not attempt to. Will was altogether different from him alike in body and mind: slimmer, longer, more graceful, a beautiful runner and jumper. But slight though he was he could out-last his thick-stemmed senior in the hay-field. His speech was slow and rare; his eyes, sweet and kind as those of a domestic animal, met yours reluctantly, almost furtively, and instantly withdrew. His hair, crisp as George's, was red-brown instead of black. He had no known vices. He was never loud or coarse, and never went a-wenching. The only thing in a skirt George had ever seen his brother with was young Esther Thorp, the vicar's daughter, in the Croft among the young stock. And she didn't count. She were gentry, she were. Besides she and Will weren't man and woman at all; they was just bairns together wi the same hobby, and there were ten years atween em.

Except when he was among his horses Will always seemed a bit out of it, a changeling, unused to earth and its ways, and obviously uneasy amongst men. In the great cart-stables, in the Croft among the brood-mares at foaling time, with the yearlings in Long-acres, he found himself. Then the clouds lifted: he was

11

at home. Will moved among his own, with hand outstretched, the kindness in his eye, making a low murmuring that was half a whistle, half a song; wordless like the trilling of a nightingale or the rumour of a brook.

CHAPTER THREE

In the Croft

Boxer and Beauty were born in the spring of 1912, within half-an-hour of each other in the Croft; as the paddock outside the homestead where the brood-mares run is called.

They were not twins, nor so far as is known any blood-connection; and they were of the type known as vanners.

When first the knotted ball of convoluted legs and wet yellow-brown fur that was some day to be Boxer began to unwind itself, and the little newcomer opened vague eyes in blank amazement, the first thing he beheld was Young Will's face, seen dim as a moon through mist, against the dark and heaving flank of his peering dam; the first voice he heard was Young Will's — a kind voice too, very soothing. As he opened his nostrils tentatively, and the flood of this astounding new experience came pouring in on him through the gateways of his senses, he snuffed, sneezed, staggered after many false starts on to tall pillar-like legs and stood there as one coming round from a long swoon, with quivering tail and the ridiculous woolly mane of the toy-horse.

Young Will thrust his thumbs, smeared with warm milk, between the gums of the foal.

"Suck away, ma lad! Tha wunna suck em off," came the pleasant voice that brought with it hope and faith, and was evidence to the shivering little stranger that this new world into which he had been plunged so suddenly was kind and welcoming.

It was a mild evening of May and Will left the two foals under the elms in the Croft with their dams for the night. Old William was standing at the gate of the yard, bulky and benevolent by reason of the beauty of the evening and still more because two foals of the type that spelt money had been born to him and Gallops.

"All right?" he asked, slobbering a peppermint.

"Aye. T' colt-foal, he's a little beauty. The filly, she's a gawk." Will laughed his awkward school-boy laughter.

"If the bone's there the beauty's there," remarked Old William laconically. It was a favourite saying with him that Gallops was built on bone.

"The bone's there," replied Young Will — "too much on it. She's a reg'lar raw-boned un, she is."

There is little variety in the names of cart-horses. From age to age the farm-stables of England have been filled with Captains and Kings, Sues and Sallies, Bouncers and Bessies; and the last cart-horse this country will ever know will probably answer to the name of Jack or Jenny.

Boxer and Beauty were never formally christened. At Gallops there was no time for poetry play-actin, as Old William called all sentiment. Of young women of leisure, who introduce this pleasant element into life, there was a plentiful lack on the farm. And the old woman scorned them. Her one aim was to get on wi' it. Drudge and drive was the order of the day with Martha Lord and her gaunt help-mates. The names of horses and cows issued some-how like bubbles out of the deeps of the con-sciousness of the community, nobody quite knew how. When Esther Thorp asked Will about the origin of the titles Boxer and Beauty, Will only shook his head.

"Who christened their names? Nobody I reckon. They just was."

Boxer and Beauty in fact were always Boxer and Beauty except when, as not seldom happened, they became Box' and Beaut', owing to the incorrigible tendency of human nature to take short cuts at any cost and save a fraction of a second's labour.

As a foal Boxer won handsomely in his class at the autumn Shire-horse Show in Barnston. Beauty, entered in the same class, did not win and was not meant to win. She was only entered at Will's request because as Mrs. Thorp put it — "wherever Boxer went Beauty had to go"; and they travelled the road with their dams better together than single. That was as true of Boxer as it was of Beauty. He was very man, and might snub Beauty brutally especially in company, but he moped when she was not with him.

At the show they made an outstanding young couple and attracted a good deal of attention, Boxer for his good looks, Beauty for her promise of power. Both were bright bays with black points, and Beauty had a white streak trickling down her face in a long crooked line to enhance her charms and help her look ridiculous.

"Make a pair some day, Will," said Mrs. Thorp.

"Ah," said Will laconically; and it was a very

favourite saying of his. But he was pleased, Esther saw.

Thereafter Boxer and Beauty grew up together in the Croft, and spent much time with their muzzles across each other's withers, musing on what the world had in store for them. Boxer was the leader in every frolic, Beauty his submissive follower. There was no doubt of Beauty's devotion; whether it was returned was another question. Boxer was very much the young male; self-contained, distinctly conceited, and undemonstrative. He accepted all the lady gave him as his due, and apparently gave little in return. Beauty was as an incorrigible sentimentalist as any plain spinster, who seeks to make up for her lack of attractiveness by faithfulness and excess of sympathy. All her life she was a lady of one love with the qualities and limitations of such an one. Her heels were ever ready for other followers in the Croft and, if her heels needed reinforcing her teeth came into play. Boxer was slightly bored by her too obvious attentions but suffered them with the irritable complacency of the spoiled darling of the drawing-room. He was now at the age when had he possessed two legs instead of four he would have oiled his hair, smoked a fag, and leaned against the wall on Sunday with his contemporaries, watching the girls go by to church, with a superior smirk.

Beauty, it is true, had much to excuse her foolishness: for there was as little doubt that Boxer was a good-looking youngster as that he knew it. The two for all their mutual sympathy differed in temperament as in physique. Boxer from a foal up was mighty particular. He would let nobody but Will handle him, and only Will and Esther Thorp approach him; while, if anybody touched his head, he made as much fuss about it as a young society belle straight from the hands of the coiffeur. On the other hand nothing upset Beauty so long as she was with her love. A child could play with her.

Boxer and Beauty were not shire-horses themselves, but they carried nearly as much feather, and were almost as massive.

Indeed like many of the vanner type both had shire-horse blood in them. Boxer owned among his ancestors Harold, and Beauty among hers Premier — those legendary champions from the Calwich stable, mighty-crested, monumental as cathedrals, whose portraits from the *Stock-keeper* and elsewhere still adorn the parlours and harness-rooms of many a farm in the Midlands and the North.

CHAPTER FOUR

The Breaking

Young cart-horses are first broken to the service of man at two years old, usually in the spring or early summer at the slack time before haying begins.

The breaking on a farm such as Gallops is a rough and ready job. There is more in it of brutality than finesse. Time is of the essence of the matter: for labour is always short, and every job done means another job, often as important, left undone.

On Gallops it involved less violence than on most farms. That was because of Young Will. Every youngster broken to bit and harness was broken by him, and had been ever since he first took on the job of horseman as quite a lad. In his own department Young Will reigned an absolute despot. There not even George dare interfere.

Will began on Boxer and Beauty as he began on all the rest. One late spring evening, with the thrushes shouting in the elms, after his day's work was done, he strolled into the Croft and called softly, seductively. The two young things came to him slowly across the shadows, Boxer as always leading, with outstretched muzzle and soft beard, pretending to be coy. In Young Will's huge pockets were hunks of the beloved cow-cake. They smelt it at once, and Boxer began to burrow and fumble for it. Beauty of course must go for the pocket Boxer was already investigating, and suffer brutal rebuff accordingly. As Boxer nosed, Will handled his head and ears, talking softly the while. The colt was too deeply engaged treasure-hunting to resent the treatment. Will now took out the cow-cake and gave it to the youngsters. As they munched he threw his arm over Boxer's neck like a collar, and then dropped it over the horse's back with the quiet thump of a harness-saddle descending. Boxer took it all patiently enough.

Young Will passed ten minutes with his pupils thus every evening for a week. And every evening after the lesson, as he returned to the yard, they followed him doubtfully and stood awhile with their heads over the gate that shut them off from the forbidden land within which they saw young Bouncer, moving like a lord, and other casual acquaintances of the Croft.

This was a favourite position of theirs and encouraged by Young Will. From there they watched the business of the great yard that some day they would share, and grew used to it: horses ready-harnessed and clanking out of the stables, Bouncer, a year their senior, giving himself the airs of a veteran teamster, the come-and-go of the great drays, the rattling of milk-cans, the bull-floats, the rakes, the binders.

"Learns em it like," Young Will told Esther Thorp, who had come up with her governess to pay the milk-bill.

A week later, as he was tramping through Birkby Whin at the head of a three-horse dray, he passed the girl swinging long-legged on the vicarage gate and paused.

"I begins em to-morrow," he told her briefly.

She slid to the ground.

"What?" she asked keenly.

"Box' and Beaut'," he answered. "Schoolin em."

"Where?"

" The Croft. Five o'clock."

She was too shy to ask for an invitation; but her eagerness was obvious.

"Like to coom?" he asked sombrely at last.

"May I?"

Will nodded.

"Best not bring *her*, I reckon. Might scarify em like — Box' especially." It was unnecessary to specify to whom the *her* referred.

"She's gone," Esther replied eagerly. "It's holidays. I'm free, thank goodness."

Will grinned.

"All right," he said, and marched off after his team, long whip on shoulder.

Next afternoon the girl turned up at Gallops punctually to the minute. Mrs. Lord, who was as fond of Esther as she was of any human being, apart from her Old William and his George, gave her tea and the barm-cakes, for which Gallops was famous, especially made for her visitor, with a superfluity of currants.

"Goin horse-breakin, aren't yo?" she said with the surly ungraciousness that was the nearest approach to good manners she could manage — "Yo and young Will?"

"I hope so."

"What's moother say?" not unkindly.

Esther laughed gaily.

"Mother did it herself when she was my age!"

It was never from mother that Esther's difficulties came.

Just then Will came by the open window with two halters and a long cart-whip. He caught the girl's eye and jerked his head.

Esther rose up and followed him out into the Croft. There were Boxer and Beauty standing together as always under an elm, Beauty her nose over Boxer's withers; and old mare Esmeralda a little apart.

Young Will strode towards them, the girl at his side. They did not speak. Few words, indeed, ever passed between them. They seemed to understand each other without speech like animals. Young Will's attitude towards the girl was much the same, in fact, as towards his horses.

"Box' first," he now said. "Beaut's all right. She'll follow him anywhere."

He gave the girl the long cart-whip and one of the halters. Then he stood still and called.

"They know you," he said. "They'll coom."

And come they did. Will without more ado slipped a halter over Boxer's head. The young horse made no trouble. To the halter a rope was attached. Will pulled on it, trying to induce Boxer to follow. But Boxer wouldn't. The unusual restraint annoyed him. Young Will, rope in hand, went in front and called. Boxer only shook his bearded head. Will leaned gently on the rope: so did Boxer. His nose came out, his neck extended, till the two were in a straight line; but his bulky young body remained obdurate. With his muzzle out and

23

his forelegs planted he looked supremely silly
and dogged.

Esther chuckled.

Young Will relaxed his pull, and turned his
sweet wise eyes, full of humour, on the girl.

"Balks," he said.

Unhitching the rope, but leaving the halter
on, he walked away, calling. After a little delib-
eration Boxer followed him, and Beauty followed Boxer.

Esther gave a little skip of delight.

"How like us!" she cried.

"Yes," said Will deliberately. "But which is
it? Doos they take after us or us after they?"

The girl pondered deeply.

"I don't think either. I think we both take
after a Third." She didn't know quite what
she meant herself; but she thought she meant
something. Anyway it was beyond Will; who
did not attempt to follow up her idea.

Attaching the rope once more, he pulled
again — with the same result.

"What shall you do now?" asked Esther.

"Force him to it," replied her companion
briefly. "Nothing for it only that."

Esther came from a liberal home and was
brimming with the ideas, educational and
Montessorian, at that time paramount.

"Pity," she said gravely.

"'Tis," Young Will admitted with equal solemnity. "Only got to be. See, there's a long way and a short way. Long way's best, but short way's shortest. I likes t' long way, I doos. But Gallops got to goo on, as dad says. And if yo're drove to short way, then it's force em to it — same as in a class at school. If yo've nobbut one scholar happen yo can take and coax him, and spend all day at it if needs be. But if yo've fifty yo canna. So farmers got to force, where gentry can coax. Cooms down to cash in the end. Most always doos in ma notion on it."

He called to the men in the yard. Two or three of them, who had been watching over the gate, came grinning. This was a bit of sport for them, much enjoyed, and relieving the monotony of hum-drum toil. They got on to the rope.

"Now for tug o war!" said Young Will, and took first place on the rope, facing Boxer. That was the post of danger. If when he said the word and the man leaned on the rope, the young horse gave way and came with a bull-rush, the first man might be trampled. Young Will had no fear. He knew from long experience that young cart-horses, clumsy though they may appear, are as delicate in their treading as thoroughbreds, and will avoid trampling a man who is down at almost any cost. In all his experience he had known but one accident and that to Long Clayton, whose feet, as Will truly pointed out at the time, yo could scarce help treadin on if yo was in same field wi him.

"Steady!" said Will. "Now — pull!"

The men behind him bore their weight on the rope, increasing their pull gently, heels in, backs slanted. Young Boxer thought it was a game. He dug his toes in and sat back. As the men straightened out, so did he. Will whistled.

"Coop, ma lad!" he called cheerily.

Boxer's ears went forward, but his body back.

Young Will nodded to Esther.

"Crack t' whip!"

The girl cracked it most effectively. Boxer leapt as though stung: the rope gave: the men staggered back: Boxer was under way before he knew it.

"Now run away wi it!" called Will.

Boxer saw the kind face backing rapidly away before him, and heard the familiar voice encouraging him. He followed reluctantly. Then he found it less trouble not to resist, and came along ungraciously, indeed, but without a fight.

Young Will left the rope, went to the colt's head, and made much of him as he followed the men suspiciously about the field.

Then Young Will was aware of another haltered head at his side. It was Beauty. Esther had slipped the halter on her head unbidden and was leading her.

Young Will looked at the long girl with quiet approval. She was like a foal herself, he thought.

"Well done," he said laconically.

"It wasn't difficult," Esther replied.

They left the halters on, and returned again next evening. To Esther this was greater fun than even the holiday at the sea of which she had been disappointed.

CHAPTER FIVE

Learning Stable

After a week, when the pair had been halter-broken and would follow readily, Young Will led Boxer into the yard. Esther followed with Beauty. Slowly round the yard they went, giving the youngsters time to admire and absorb the strange new objects — the water-cart, the milk-float, the many-legged binding-machine that looked like some monstrous insect and required much sniffing.

Then Will led Boxer to the door of the stable.

The young horse peered into the dimness with alert ears and wide sensing nostrils. He had never seen anything like that before. The half-light frightened him and made him tremble. It was a dungeon too, he saw, with walls, from which, once you were in it, there was no escape. He tossed up his head and backed away into Beauty, who was at his heels. The sense of her presence, and the familiar dig of her muzzle into his quarters, reassured him somewhat. His eyes explored the dungeon with increasing curiosity and diminishing fear. From it arose a fragrant smell and the sound of munching. Then as his eyes became accustomed to the half-light he was aware of a long row of horses, each in a little cell to himself. They were prisoners, but they were busy, and they were obviously happy. The steady sound of their munching, and the muffled stir of their occasional movements, thrilled Boxer. He was desperately intrigued. What were they eating so enjoyably? Fear and curiosity battled in his heart, and curiosity won. He poked his nose in further and recognised young Bouncer, a year his senior, who had left the Croft six months since, but still sometimes stalked across it, sober as a judge, with an air of majesty, in clanking armour, far too uplifted to notice old friends.

Bouncer was standing beside an empty stall, too absorbed in enjoying his meal to pay attention to the new boy. That empty stall was immediately opposite Boxer.

"Coop," said Will firmly and slipped his hand up to Boxer's chin. "Coom then."

Boxer entered delicately. His feet rang on the tiles, and he trembled violently. But Will was leading the way into the cell, and there was

Bouncer in his cell alongside, munching away as contented as you please, and Beauty pushing eagerly behind; while that delicious fragrance enticed and tempted him.

He entered the cell. The floor was soft to his feet, brown as beech-mast, and very fragrant and comforting. He snuffled it with his muzzle only to find it was not good to eat. Will was patting him and fastening his head-rope to the ring of the manger.

Beauty followed behind. Of course she wanted to squeeze into the same stall as Boxer, but Esther wrestled with her.

"Mind she doesna bang thee agin t' stall-post!" called Will warningly.

He slipped out of Boxer's stall and fended the mare off into the next stall, throwing the whole of his weight against her shoulder. She ranged up alongside Boxer, just the wooden partition between them. Boxer could hear her rubbing against it.

Then he was seized with panic. He flung up his head to get away from the restraining head-rope. As he did so he was aware of Bouncer's yellow teeth grinning at him over the top of the partition on the left. At the same moment Beauty whinnied, that soft smothered whinny of hers he knew so well. Boxer answered her in the same muffled tone. She put up her muzzle. So did he. The two kissed over the wall that divided them, and they were comforted.

Just at that moment a miracle happened. A bundle of gold tumbled down from heaven into the manger at Boxer's nose. He jumped and sweated. Then he was aware that it was from this mass of gold that the alluring fragrance, which on entering had intoxicated him, came flooding. It was old hay, very sweet. He plunged his nose into it and forgot his fears.

Man and girl, standing behind, looked at each other. Then Will laughed.

"Got him," he said.

For two days Boxer and Beauty stayed in their stalls, "learning stable", as Young Will called it. They became accustomed to men passing down the gang-way behind them, to drinking water from buckets, to the feet in the loft overhead, the horses clanking out to work, the mucking-out of their stalls. At first they were restless. They missed the open and the great calm heavens above and about them, Boxer especially. Sometimes he became afraid. The restraint terrified him. At night he would think he was suffocating: for there were no stars, so that it was like a grave. Then he shifted on his great feet, snuffled, and sweated. But the movements of Bouncer and Beauty on either side steadied him: and if he tended to become frantic Beauty's muzzle would appear over the partition, calm and mothering, to inquire what the trouble was. Young Will spent ten minutes with them every day, morning and evening, talking to them. So did Esther.

On the third evening Will told the girl he should turn them out again next day.

"Learned em their A. B. C. like," he said. "Back to play now. All work and no play makes Jack a dull boy."

Esther turned up next evening as he knew she would.

To get the young horses out seemed a simple enough operation; but like everything else to do with the handling of animals it required tact and tactics.

"I'll take Box' first," said Young Will. "Beaut' 'll follow anywhere, but she willna lead, Beaut' willna. Mind she doesna rush thee, nor hit herself."

He led Boxer out into the yard. For a moment the glare seemed to confuse and flurry the young horse. He stood uncertain. Then the pure fresh air rushed in on him, flooding his senses. It was a second birth. Will slipped the halter. The gate into the Croft was open. Boxer, ungallantly refusing to wait for his lady, made a clumsy rush for liberty.

Will watched him with a grin.

Just then George, standing in the door of the farm, shouted at him. He turned swiftly.

Esther had not understood that she was to wait and had been following with the mare. Beauty, mad to be after her love, and suffering from the same excitement as Boxer, came blundering through the door, and threw the girl against it. She was flung to her knees but hung on to the halter bravely. Will leapt to her help, seized the halter, and slipped it. Beauty careered away after Box' with a great clatter of hoofs.

George came up.

"That's dangerous, that is," he said censoriously.

Will had helped the girl to her feet.

"Yo leave that to me," he said sullenly. "I know my hörses."

George turned away.

"Yo'll have an accident yet, yo will," he said.

"I will if I'm interfered wi," retorted Will doggedly. "That's sure."

His eyes met Esther's, which were dancing. Her hair was tumbled, but she was the only one of the three who had not been frightened.

Together man and girl watched Boxer and Beauty careering round the field with clumsy buckings and lashing heels.

"They've finished their 'prentice'," said Young Will. "Like lads they be let out o school. Shan't touch em again now till back-end."

CHAPTER SIX

At the Plough

Before Boxer and Beauty went to school again the cloudburst of blood had deluged Europe.

Nothing escaped, not even Gallops.

George was one of the first to go to the War. He told his father his decision over a pipe in the great kitchen where they all sat after the day's work.

"If England goos down, Gallops goos with it, I reckon," said George. "That's how I figures it out."

The old man was troubled and shewed it as always by rising to his feet and stumping about the room.

"England willna go down nor won't Gallops," he grunted, waddling up and down in his slippers.

"It will if we doesna fight for it, I reckon."

"And what'll I do for foreman?" asked Old William abruptly.

George puffed.

"There's Young Will."

The old man snorted.

"Will! He's nobbut a horse-man. 'Tis a foreman Gallops wants."

"There's more in Will nor what tha' knows, dad," answered George, with the shrewdness, amounting almost to vision, that made him the man he was. "Give him his chance. He'll grow to it. It's me's kep him back likely."

So George went; and his mother's heart went with him. She disliked Young Will all the more because he took his brother's place. In Martha Lord's view her second son wasn't rightly right; and she had no use for weaklings whether in the house or on the farm. The proper way to deal wi such was the way folks dealt wi em in old days; as she still dealt with an unsatisfactory puppy or an unwanted kitten — send em back where they coom fra'.

But Will justified his brother's choice. He was not a George, but responsibility developed him, even as George had predicted. His method was very different from his brother's, but he carried on soom gait, so that his father was satisfied, and his mother disagreeably surprised. But he made no secret of the fact that his home was in the stable and his heart still with his horses, especially Boxer and Beauty.

"Thinks the world of Box' and Beaut', Will do," the men said.

"Thinks ower much of em to ma reckoning," commented Old William sourly.

It was not however till the harvest was well over, and the first frosts whitening the morning fields, that Young Will took up afresh the task of educating the young pair.

One afternoon Esther Thorp coming up to the farm with her mother, and peeping into the cart-stable, found Boxer and Beauty back in their old stalls. But they were standing on the pillar-reins now, their heads where their tails should be, collars on and head-stalls, traces curled, the heavy harness-saddles on their backs, absorbed in champing their bits.

"Mouthing em," Young Will explained to the girl. "Colt-bits they be. See, there's play-things on em — toys we calls em." He took down a colt-bit from the wall and shewed the girl the loose steel tassels that swivelled freely on the barrel of the bit. "It amuses em to work em wi their tongues. That makes em drop their chins and bends their neck. Learns em without their knowing it like."

"How long does *that* lesson go on, Will?" asked Mrs. Thorp.

"Keep em at it twenty-four hours wi bits in

their mouths. Then give em a spell. And after that take em and try em in the roller," answered Will.

"When will that be?" asked Esther.

"To-morrow. Five o'clock.' He glanced at the girl. "Wouldst' like to coom?"

"Rather," replied Esther eagerly. "May I, mum?"

Mrs. Thorp laughed.

"You've got no lessons of your own, my dear, at present," she said. "So you may as well give lessons to others." She explained to Will that her daughter was to have gone to Paris that autumn to finish her education, but the War had frustrated that plan as it had millions of other plans.

Young Will nodded.

"If she cooms I shan't need a lad." He moved off. "To-morrow then. Five. Cant Thorns."

The long-legged girl hopped away rejoicing on her mother's arm.

She was waiting next day at Cant Thorns when Will came along leading Boxer. The young horse was fully accoutred now, stepping gravely, and self-conscious as a girl who has just put up her hair. Beauty could be heard back in the stable whinnying for her mate.

A lad followed with old Esmeralda, the seventeen-hand mare, used always for break-

ing because of her bulk and bony promontories.

Esmeralda was put in the shafts of the roller,
and Boxer harnessed outside. Young Will took
the lines, as he called the reins, and Esther the
lunging rope.

Will clucked and gurgled in his throat; and
Esmeralda moved forward with the deliberate
reluctant action of a Mauretania gathering way.

The inexorable roller came on Boxer's heels.
He leapt forward into his collar; the chains
snapped taut; and he was brought up with
violence. Esmeralda, justifiably annoyed at the
jerk, snatched at her companion's head, and
let him feel some of her promontories.

"Coop, Boxer, coop!" came the soothing
voice from behind.

The girl at the young horse's side laid her
hand on his neck. Esmeralda moved on like a
tide. Boxer sweated.

The clanking Thing-Behind drove him forward: the vice about his shoulders held him
back. There was no escape to the right because
of Esmeralda's huge bulk; and bonds pre-
vented him breaking away to the left. To walk
sedately, adjusted between the two forces, fore
and aft, and without being buffeted, was difficult; but it could be done. Esmeralda clearly
did it. Boxer found the secret with amazing
speed under the pressure of necessity. It was

a simple secret too. If you walked fast enough, and not too fast, leaning gently against the Thing-in-Front, then the Thing-Behind followed pleasantly and without pain and let you alone. Moreover when you did this aright you derived a satisfactory sense of power and the comfort that arises from fulfilling your natural function aright. That was a new and pleasant experience to the young horse.

At the end of two hours Boxer was leaning steadily against his collar like an old teamster, and already beginning to answer to Will's voice. He had conquered something and made it his own; and with his new accomplishment had come an access of conceit.

Will pulled up, got down from his perch, and came and talked to the young horse.

"Wonderful how quick they takes to it," he said dreamily to his companion. "Bred in em, I suppose — same as the children o scholars lappin up their letters like milk. In the blood like, time out o mind."

Things were changing fast at Gallops now and, indeed, throughout the world. George had long gone. Early in 1915 Esther Thorp followed, her father leaving Birkby Whin for a Derbyshire parish. But War or no War Gallops had to carry on. Harvest and seedtime, breaking and mating, would tarry for no man.

Boxer and Beauty had joined the ranks of the toilers, and settled steadily down to their life-work. From the roller they passed to the plough, and laboured faithfully for a year at that primordial task of their kind, at first with old mare Esmeralda to teach and steady them, and later together.

In the autumn Old William came and looked at the youngsters working in the Went. He was secretly amazed: for it is seldom that a pair of three-year olds are steady enough to work together thus. But he was far too much Old William either to comment or praise.

"Yo've got em together then," said the old man as the plough stopped at the end of a furrow, and Boxer and Beauty came lurching round, slow and patient and utterly amenable to Will's gurgled objurgations. The manœuvre executed the horse-man paused.

"Ah," he said and added after a lengthy pause — "They works best so, I reckon. Steadies em. Like man and wife, Box' and Beaut'."

"More like father and two children," replied Old William. "There's three of you by all accounts."

There was the familiar touch of shrewishness in his voice. He thought Will spent too much time on his horses for the foreman of Gallops, and most of all on Boxer and Beauty.

Young Will felt the implied criticism and resented it.

"They works best for me," he said curtly. "I can get more out of em."

That shot if any would hit the old man between wind and water, he knew. Unfortunately it ricocheted and struck the firer.

"So I hears," grunted Old William. "That Box' willna work for nobody but you, Ned tells me."

Ned was the head stable-lad. He did not like Boxer, and the head-horseman accordingly did not like him.

Young Will resumed the handle of his plough, polished with the sweat of generations of grimy hands.

"I wouldna bother what Ned says," he grumbled. "That's the way trouble cooms."

Old William, his eyes screwed up against the westering sun, stood up against the hedge with puckered lips. Will had been impertinent and needed a tap.

"Sell em a pair happen when time cooms," he said in a quiet smothered voice that spelt *Beware!* to those who knew him.

Dumb and glum, Will turned, and gurgling in his throat set his wise and gentle children of the plough going afresh.

Old William rolled away, grinning covertly. Will was a good lad on the whole, and champion at his job, but he had one sad weakness: he couldn't a-bear to part wi his horses, not when sellin time coom, though they was ripe for it. But Will must just put up wi it. Gallops got to goo on. That was the one stable point in a world in flux.

CHAPTER SEVEN

George

Early in 1916 George came home on leave for the first time since he had gone to France. Changed himself he found everything changing, even Gallops.

The young men were being drawn off the land into the trenches, and the girls taking their places. But the greatest change of all was in George himself. Young Will, the quietly observant, noticed that at once. George was unhappy. That staggered Will because it was something so new — George, the efficient, the successful, unhappy, almost moping, for the first time in his life.

All his life George had been a whirring cog in a swiftly humming machine and had found his joy in speed. Now he had come to a halt. He wasn't getting on himself, neither was the War so far as he could see.

"They doesn't seem to get along wi it, not to ma way o thinkin any road," he told his listeners over the fire at night. "Hold-up all the way round."

He didn't like the War and didn't pretend to: he wasn't doing any good himself and didn't believe anybody else was: none the less he was in it and meant to go through with it. No shirking about George however miserable he might be.

He walked round the farm but with none of the old brisk vigour, ordering this and that. He was remote, self-absorbed, slow in his speech and movements. Will was unhappy because of George's unhappiness. It was not that the two had ever been intimate: it was rather that Will, the most natural of living creatures, thought there was something, unnatural, forced, abominable about George being so unlike himself.

Once the elder brother found the younger ploughing with Boxer and Beauty.

He watched the three at work for some time.

"They're coomin on nice," he said at last, with that gentleness which was one of his new characteristics.

"Aye," replied Will. "Wearin down to it, I reckon. Two year at the plough this backend. Then try em atween the shafts, I suppose."

"If dad don't sell first," said George.

45

"Is he talkin of it?" asked Will, rousing instantly as to the touch of a whip.

"Nay, I don't know as he is," George replied. "But horses fetch their price these days — vanners anyway. Artillery yo see."

George had obviously made the remark innocently and without malicious intent. Will saw that at once and took some comfort from it.

"There's time yet," he said. "They're nobbut four off. Give em till seven. Reckon they'll fetch more then."

George nodded.

"Yo're right," he said, but added with a shrewd kindliness in a warning note — "But yo won't have em for always, Will." Like his father he was aware of his brother's weakness, and thought his fondness for the pair was becoming an obsession which would harm him.

"I'll have them for now any road," Will retorted sharply. He flopped the lines — "Gee, Box'! Woa, Beaut'! — Whoop! — Steady!"

That was in the spring of 1916. Three months later George was killed on the Sommie, as they called it in the village, speaking the word to rhyme with Tommy, in a War in which he no longer believed and in a cause he had come to doubt.

46

That stunned Young Will. He couldn't believe that George was dead — George of all men! — *George!* Will used to lie awake through the September nights in his little room at the end of the passage puzzling over it. George lying there so quiet under a sprinkling of earth — never so much as a kick in him!

Will would rise up on his elbows in his narrow bed and stare out at the deep and star-shod night. One thing sure: George wouldn't like it. He'd fight, old George would, yo could lay to that. Always fought, George did, when he got what he hadn't asked for. Poor old George! Not that Will blamed the Germans entirely, as he told his solitary intimate, the village school-master: he knew old George too well for that.

"Brought his trouble on his own head like, I expect," he said with that mixture of innocence and shrewdness which was characteristic of him. "See where it was, George *could* be spiteful. And if the Germans got interferin wi him when he was doin a job o work, like as not he'd smack out at em. And they mightn't like that and spite him back."

And if Will took George's death hard, Old William and his wife were heart-broken. Martha Lord didn't weep: it might have been better if she had. But she showed herself as aggrieved and resentful as a cow robbed of its calf by the butcher, she doesn't know why; and she made it clear that she held Will responsible for his brother's death.

Will knew that, and accepted it philosophically.

"She got to work it off on somebody, I suppose," he told his confidante. "And me better'n the wenches. See mother thinks it were me." He gazed away into the autumn evening with steady penetrating eyes — "It weren't though," he added with quiet confidence.

Unlike his wife, Old William took what was for him a death-blow very quietly, dreadfully so. Lord Gord seemed to have forgotten how to lose his temper. All the hands noticed it.

"The boss has fairly took it," they muttered. "Main bad he be."

Then one evening at dusk he came labouring up to Will in the stable, breathing heavily.

"Tha' mun marry now, Will," he said huskily.

Will mucked about with the fork.

"I reckon so," he answered moodily.

Old William waddled back to his wife, shaking his head.

"He doesna like it," he told her.

"I daresay he doesna," snapped Martha. "But he's got to put oop wi what he doesna like same as pore George and a sight more of em. Why should Will have it all his own way?"

"His heart's wi his horses" said Old William. "That's where it is. But he'll do it, I reckon — for Gallops' sake."

CHAPTER EIGHT

A Hay-bay

But there was another job of work Will thought he ought to put through now George was dead, before he got on with the marrying.

He was not a fighting-man by temperament, but he was twenty-eight now, and he had a vague feeling in his heart that he ought to take the place his brother had left vacant in the trenches. So much he owed to George and Gallops. The country and the cause were hardly present in his consciousness. He didn't want to go: he had no wish whatever to avenge George: above all he didn't want to leave his horses. But there was an always growing urge of the spirit, a welling up in the tidal waters of subconsciousness, pushing him on however reluctantly towards the inevitable. The feeling was perhaps all the stronger because Ern, the next brother, had gone up and been rejected: Will had always known Ern would be — touched in the wind, Ern were: *a roarer*, Will called him; while Boy Hal, the baby of the family, was still at school. Will had already been turned down himself once, but not on the ground of health. He had registered duly under Lord Derby's scheme late in 1915, but had never been called up. When he had presented himself before the recruiting-officer in Barnston and testified his willingness to go, that worthy had turned to his files.

"What name?"

"William Lord."

"Lord of Gallops?"

"I believe so."

The other had shaken his head.

"Foreman aren't you? — Eight hundred acres. Can't do better than where you are." The food-supply of the country was growing daily more precarious, the submarines always more effective.

That had satisfied Will at the time. But now George was dead it was different.'

When the corn was harvested, he told his father his intention. The old man did and said exactly what he had done and said just two years before when George had come to him with the same story. He lifted heavily out of his chair, and shuffled about the room in his slippers.

"What about me and Gallops?' he barked.

Young Will smiled his stubborn smile that the old man knew meant he was not to be argued out of his decision.

"Reckon Gallops 'll goo on soom gait," he said. "Got too.'

Old William accepted the inevitable because he had to, and gave Young Will leave off for two nights.

"Mind and coom back," the old man urged him.

"I'll coom back," answered Will. "I'm nobbut goin to have a chat wi em."

He went to the door of the cart-stable, saw that Boxer and Beauty were happily munching side by side, stood for a moment with downcast eyes listening with a pleased expression to what was for him the most soothing music in the world — a dozen horses champing their corn in unison after a good day's work; and then went off on his business.

He was not unhappy: for he had a plan in his head, one of those simple, cunning plans on which the innocent of earth so pride themselves.

Next day, however, when he appeared before the Tribunal he found them difficult, obstructive. The food-situation was causing always graver anxiety.

The chairman asked Will what he wanted to do if they did let him go.

Will smiled his awkward smile of a yokel.

"Well, I reckon I might be head-horseman to one o they girt 'tillery batteries — howitzers, they calls em, I believe."

The military representative shook his head.

"There's no such job."

"Who sees to the horses then?" asked Will, gentle as he was dogged. "Somebody must, I suppose."

"The officers," replied the other.

Young Will was crestfallen. The last thing in the world he wanted was to be an officer; but he did want his own way.

"What d'yo want for that?" he asked.

"For what?'

"To be an officer in the 'tillery."

"Sums," replied the soldier briefly.

Young Will snickered. Memories of his school-days and trouble with his arithmetic crowded in on him.

"That beats me," he said; but he was not done yet.

A look of cunning came into his sweet brown eyes.

"Happen I might bring a team or two along o me," he said.

The bribe proved ineffectual. He was told to go back to his farm.

As he slouched out the military representative said to him with a grin.

"I can't take you, Lord; but I might take your horses."

Will stopped dead.

"Tha' willna!" he cried. "If I don't go neether won't my hörses."

The soldier smirked.

"Next time I'm Gallops-way I'll look you up," was all he said.

Will marked the smirk and abandoning his second night's leave hastened home in something like a panic.

He was not happy until he saw Boxer and Beauty side by side much as he had left them — but not quite. Something had happened in his absence. He was aware of it as instantly as a nurse, away an hour, is aware that something has disturbed her charge. Boxer was on edge, all ears and eyes and startled movements. His manger showed that he was off his feed too, and his coat that he was ruffled. The sweat had dried on it. Will went up to him in his stall and talked to him. Boxer was almost pathetically glad to see him. He nuzzled up against him, and rubbed his head against the familiar shoulder.

"What's coom to Box' then?" he said sharply

to one of the men in the yard as he left the stable.

"Him and Ned got bashin', I believe," the other answered.

The head stable-lad, it seemed, had put the horse in the manure-cart.

"Who told him put Box' in the manure-cart?" flared Will.

It was seldom Will flared: in that matter he was utterly unlike George who was a regular Christmas cracker for goin off pop just when yo didn't expect it; but when Will *did* flare he went very funny wi it — very funny indeed.

Will's informant shook his head warily. He couldna say to be sure. All he could say was that there had been a bit of a hay-bay. Box' had took mad and throw'd himself about the yard a caution.

Will heard more of the incident that evening from Old William, who was in the worst of tempers.

"That Box' o yourn's queer," he told Will. "Broke ma cart; broke 'isself; and nigh broke Ned."

"He's all right wi me," answered Will sulkily.

His father turned on him savagely.

"And what's good o that to Gallops?" he shouted. "If he'll only work for you?'

"Box' is none so bad if he's handled proper," muttered Young Will.

"I'll have to get shut of him," said Old William morosely. "That's short of it."

"Let him coom on a bit first, dad," said Will soothingly. "He's all the while a-growin into mooney."

Young Will made it his business to get to the bottom of the trouble in the yard. He had little difficulty: for Lowndes, the head cowman, disliked the head stable-lad who had thrown over his daughter after taking advantage of her. Boxer it seemed hadn't been the only one who took mad. Ned had took mad too. Then Box' r'ared oop like a girt old bear and struck out hearty. Thereon Ned oop wi his bat and smote Box' something crool over the nob.

Examination of Boxer's poll confirmed this part of the story.

Will went out, white with rage, found Ned and gave him first a hiding and then the sack; and that though stable-lads in England were becoming as rare as gold nuggets at the time.

Old William raged; but nothing would move Will.

"Him or me," he told his father.

So there was little more to be said: for Will was Gallops now. Ned required an apology, damages, and a further colossal rise in wages — if he was to be mollified and stay.

None of these were forthcoming. Young Will was as firm about the apology as Old William proved about the rise. Then happily Ned was taken away for the War. But that didn't assuage the old man's anger.

"It's that Boxer," he told his wife. "He's like a little idol to Will. Nobody dursen't touch him."

"Heathen I call it," snapped Martha Lord. "Takin on over a dumb animal as if he was a christian'd child."

To Will she remarked, at her most venomous,

"Who'll you get for stable-lad now?"

"Yo leave that to me," Will answered grumpily.

He had no notion what he should do. But he had a vague feeling that things would come out all right in the end. They usually did.

CHAPTER NINE

Will's Courting

Young Will knew very well that both his father and mother bore him a grudge in the matter; and with a stroke of something akin to genius, he atoned for his default suddenly, surprisingly, in the only way that could have satisfied them and squared the account.

It was one Sunday evening shortly after the row, as they sat round after supper in the great kitchen that Will made the announcement which reinstated him in his father's eyes. Will, it was noticed, was in his Sundays and looking smug for once and a little shy. An observer of boys, who happened to know that Will was a boy and nothing more, could have told you for certain that he was hugging a rather naughty secret.

"I done it, dad," he said at last and sniggered.

Old William, sitting big-bodied and unbuttoned, smoked.

"Done what?"

Will stared into the fire.

"Asked her."

Old William breathed deep. His wife looked up sharply over her spectacles. She was quicker in the uptake than the old man.

"Who?" she asked.

"Her that's daughter to him at the mill."

Martha Lord put down her work.

"That Milly Emmett?" she snarled. "Yo couldna well ha chose worse."

Young Will tilted back in his chair to meet his mother's attack.

"She's a woman ain't she?" he said mildly. "What more doest' want?"

There the conversation ended. Old William, deeply excited though he was, refused to show emotion before his wife. That night though he came waddling along to Will's room in the gable-end and shut the door behind him secretly.

"Why her, Will?" the old man asked in a whisper.

"Bone," Will answered.

Old William nodded encouragingly, and Young Will elaborated. The old man's excitement was infectious.

"Well ribb'd oop," said Will. "Deep through

same as I like em. And sooch 'ips and 'ocks on her!" He was mildly stirred himself now. "Should throw a good un or two if make and shape's owt."

Old William grunted approval. Of late he had more than once told his wife that Will was not the fool soom folks thought him.

"Summat i' that," he admitted to his son.

"She's a gawk — like ma Beaut'," Will continued. "But she's a good un to work."

He was quite warming up now.

"Ever see her run up t' ladder to the mill wi a hundud-weight o corn on her back, dad?"

The old man shook his head.

"Not as I knows on."

Will's eyes glowed.

"I did tho — on the way to market last Wednesday. Stopped the dray, and slipped in and asked her theer and then."

It never occurred to the old man to ask what answer the heir of Gallops received. That was understood.

The alliance, so full of promise and romance in the outset, unhappily did not appear to prosper. That was a pity, because it was the one thing that might have brought mother and son together. Martha Lord knew very well that her son was not one of the marrying sort, and that the sacrifice he was making was made for Gallops. That touched her so long as she thought that Will was serious in his intentions.

Unhappily she was unable to think it long.

Will never went near his fiancée, and she never came up to Gallops. Old William may not have remarked that, but he did notice that Will ceased to haunt the kitchen of evenings.

"Is he wi her?" he once asked his wife.

"Not him," sneered Martha. "He's in stable along o that there blessed Box'."

"He don't want to marry," muttered Old William. "His heart's wi his hörses. There's no sex in him. That's the trouble."

"Will's not a man," said his mother darkly. "I always knew how it were wi him, ever since he were a bit of a bairn."

Martha did not let her erring son off scot-free, you may be sure. As she often said *she* was not one of the milk-and-milds, whoever else might be.

"Where's Milly?" she asked him sharply one evening.

"Gone wi another chap, I did hear tell," answered Will casually. "Sergeant-major in the East Yorks or summat."

"And I don't blame her," snapped his mother, "the road yo treated her. Any girl wi a spirit in her would. Lettin her be all the time, ne'er a word nor a way wi her! Pretty make o man to win a wench, artna? As lief mate wi a dead-alive tombstone."

"Well," said Will, aggrieved. "I doesna blame her myself for that matter. I doesna blame no one. I told her I'd take and marry her if so be I got to. But I wouldna walk her and I wouldna waist her. No time for foolin and flummoxin these days, War and all."

"That's a funny way to talk," said his mother. "Why marry at all then?"

Will rose surlily and slouched out.

"Gallops got to goo on, I suppose," he said.

A day or two later Mrs. Lord brought back news from market that Milly had married her Sergeant-major.

Will was relieved, his father furious.

"Lost your wife and not found me a stable-lad," he shouted. "Makin a fool o Gallops afore em all!"

Will had tried a land-girl in place of the missing Ned but had found her useless. In consequence he had to be head stable-lad himself, in addition to being head-horseman and foreman.

"I'll find stable-lad never fear," he answered confidently, much cheered now that he was free of encumbrances. "As to wife reckon she can wait till War's over."

"Which is never!" muttered Old William.

CHAPTER TEN

Horseman's Lad

At that juncture the gods proved kind to Young Will, who was himself kind to everybody except those who abused his horses.

Esther Thorp wrote. She was nearly eighteen now and anxious to play her part in the War that had robbed her of a brother. Her mother would not let her nurse; and she refused to work in a factory or office. Her heart was set upon the land. Would they find her a job at Gallops?

Esther was one of the few human beings for whom Mrs. Lord cherished a genuine kindness. She approached Old William, who for once consulted his foreman. Young Will's heart leapt at the thought of having his old playmate back again; but he was far too cunning to say much, lest his weight thrown over violently into the scale should tilt his mother's balance against the girl.

"Got to put up wi what we can get these days, I reckon," he said to his father with an ungraciousness quite foreign to his nature.

Esther came. Young Will went in to meet her at Birkby Whin station.

When she got out of the train, he was standing on the platform in his shabby working clothes with the same kind long face, sunbrowned, the little moustache, the sweet wise eyes with the humour in them, that she knew so well. It was two-and-a-half years since the two had met. The leggy girl had become a young woman: she had broadened, deepened. Her hair was not bobbed in the fashion of the other land-girls. Brown, inclined to ruffle and stray like the mane of a wild pony, a yellow comb thrust into its tangled deeps, it was done in the simplest way, revealing the rounded beauty of a singularly shapely head. She had the same high carriage as of old, the same sensitive mouth, and lovely tilted upper lip, the same deep voice emerging astonishingly from her slim young chest, the same shy and steadfast eyes of slate-grey under a forehead that showed all the more massive because of the length and fineness of the lower face.

"Remember me, Miss?" said Young Will with a sheepish grin.

"*Rather!*" the girl replied; and he knew at once that she was still the unconscious child of nature he had parted from early in 1915.

Arrived at the farm he took her, not to see his father and mother, but straight into the stable.

"That's them," he said briefly, and waited.

"What a topper!" cried Esther, going up to Boxer in his stall.

Will answered nothing, but his kind shy eyes were radiant. And he had some cause for pride. Boxer stood sixteen and a-half hands: a handsome great horse, all bay with black points, upstanding yet compact, and pleasantly proud of himself.

He received the attentions of the girl with kindly condescension.

"He's a bit particular wi soom," murmured Young Will in the soft cooing voice that denoted he was happy. "But he remembers you. I know'd he would."

"How he's come on!" murmured the girl, pressing her cheek against the great horse's soft snuffling muzzle.

"He's five coom May," remarked Young Will. "Coomin into his pride. Pretty nigh scholarded by now is Box', only for the road."

"What's happened to Bouncer?" asked Esther.

There was a pause.

"Killed on the Sommie, I did hear, along o our George," Will answered at last.

At that moment Old William entered the stable fussily.

"Yo shouldn't let her go up to him i' t' stall, Will," he scolded. "He's funny-tempered that horse, Miss."

"He's got nothin agin her," Will answered gently. "He remembers her, doos Box'. Hörses got good memories — better'n some folks, I reckon. They never forgets them as handled em young."

There was never any question what Esther's place upon the farm should be. Young Will absorbed her from the start. The girl became stable-lad at first, and head stable-lad shortly. As such her work lay mainly with the head-horseman and his team.

Boxer and Beauty were her special care. She mucked them out, fed and groomed them, and in time harnessed even Boxer. Her deep voice, her firm handling, quite obviously soothed his restless spirit. The great horse not only tolerated the girl, but in time grew to look for her. The men and lads in the stable who had never done for Box' themselves, except when compelled to, were secretly surprised and perhaps a little jealous that the girl should succeed where they had failed. Boxer, she found, had an established reputation as a difficult, if not a dangerous, horse; and to be just to the men he had earned it. But Esther had the mysterious horse-man's way with her, inborn and not to be acquired, which conquers by understanding. Moreover she soon discovered that there was no vice in Boxer. He suffered merely like certain individuals of a higher genus from excess of temperament, and was far too generous in spirit to be spiteful. Soon after Esther's arrival therefore Young Will for the first time since the breaking of Box' was free to leave the handling of his favourite in the stable to another. Old William didn't approve. He shook his head, but he said nothing. Gallops was going on: that was his main concern.

The old man thought in his heart that the girl was in danger; but Will in fact was careful to see she ran no risks. Whatever he might allow her to do for the horse in the stable, he always worked Boxer himself, usually in a pair with Beauty, sometimes with old Esmeralda or a third horse.

"Yo've coom just right," Young Will told the girl.

Corn-drilling and ploughing of the hedge-bottoms was beginning, and those are jobs that the head-horseman usually, and Young Will invariably, did himself. He always took his lad with him as he led his team a-field.

The sacks of seed-corn were dumped along the hedge-side, and the lad was kept busy filling the skeps* from the sacks and keeping the drill supplied. When the ground was rough she walked beside the drill and saw that the feed-pipes ran and the coulters did not block.

In the drill Boxer and Beauty worked side by side. When the ploughing of the hedge-bottoms was forward they were harnessed tandem-wise, Boxer always in the lead. On these occasions Esther led him, her job being to see that he kept his head well into the hedge. Of wont in such cases the horse-man's lad has his work cut out to make the leader pull his weight. It was the other way with Boxer. Always a great worker he flung into his collar, a young giant rejoicing in his strength, as if his one passion was to escape pursuing Beauty; and as Beauty's solitary aim in life was to get nearer to Boxer, both horse-man and lad were kept busy. But the four enjoyed themselves and understood each other in a way not often given to toilers here.

Sometimes Old William came and watched the work with an approving eye.

"Quite the horse-man, Miss," he would say, and the girl's pulse would quicken, for Lord Gord was chary enough with his praise.

* Large flat-bottomed tin basins with two handles.

The head-horseman and his lad rarely spoke, though they might be in the fields together at the tail of the plough for an eight-hours' day. Sometimes she would lift her eyes and look at Will, grave and unconscious and absorbed in his work. She was never to forget him as she saw him thus, standing beside his horses, in his shirt-sleeves if the sun was shining, a sack about his shoulders if it was mizzling, in the breeches and gaiters that were the insignia of his position as a farmer's son, with his grave kind face, and the eyes in which innocence and shrewdness mingled.

Later in the year, at hay and harvest, the head-horseman, his lad, and team, worked together in a way to wring reluctant admiration even from Lord Gord.

"Soom gal," he said to Young Will of his lad, using the expressive epithet introduced into England from America during the War.

"Aye, she can do most owt wi Box'," answered Will. He never missed a chance of saying a word, apparently casual, in fact deeply calculated, on behalf of his favourite, especially to his father.

It was true too; and the old man had the evidence of it before his eyes that summer and autumn whenever he passed through the yard or walked abroad among his workers.

He would see Esther leading the great bay

out of the stable, quiet as a lamb, and powerful as a traction-engine. When the rake or the binder was at work in Long Acres or High Pastures she would ride the near horse, who was always Boxer, if Will was driving the pair, or the lead-horse, who was likewise Boxer, if he was using three, harnessed unicorn-wise. And the young horse was sedate with her and steady as a veteran of twenty summers.

CHAPTER ELEVEN

Esther

Esther found complete satisfaction in her work and her horses. Intellectually lazy in spite of excellent parts, she would spend her Sundays in utterest content lolling in the stable on a truss of hay, brooding over her horses as later in life she would squat on the floor of her nursery and brood over her babes.

Even her playtime was spent among her charges.

One evening after work Old William was horrified to see her in the Croft the centre and objective, so it seemed to him, of a charge of careering cart-horses, turned loose for a spell after a long day at the collar.

He bundled to her rescue, brandishing his stick and shouting.

Then out of the tumult of hairy creatures, nibbing, nagging, kicking, and squealing, he was aware of Esther in her worn breeches and gaiters, smiling at him as she fed her children with lumps of the adored cow-cake out of the vast pockets of her blue apron.

The girl was quick to pick up horse-language, clucking out unintelligible phrases in best Yorksheer, familiar to her from baby-hood, in a manner to bring twinkles to the eyes of the sun-browned harvesters who heard her.

"Gee back!" in deep, gurgling voice. "Whoop, steady! Gee, Box'! Steady! Arve! Coom back!"

And she did it all with a grave-eyed unconsciousness that would have made any man but Young Will fall headlong in love with her.

Mrs. Lord watched the girl all through that summer with sharp-eyed interest. She never detected in her what she sought, and indeed would have liked to find: for if Martha Lord cared little for Young Will she was ambitious and obsessed with the passion, fiercer even than her husband's, that Gallops should go on. And Gallops now meant Young Will: Ernie was good for nowt i' this world; he was funny i' the lungs, Ernie were, and had been sent away to a sanatorium on the coast to die, if all went well, at great expense to Gallops; while Boy Hal, if he came back from the War to which he had been called that summer, meant, his mother knew, to desert the land for the towns and go clerking.

Therefore Martha Lord observed Esther with covetous eye; marking with approval her tirelessness, her supple limbs, her neat and graceful figure, her easy walk.

"She's the one for Gallops," she confided to her husband. And it was characteristic of her attitude to life that she did not say "for Will."

Old William, panting about the room as he undressed, shook his head.

"She's not for Will, not even if Will was for her, which he isna."

Martha Lord was the most democratic of women when it suited her purpose and her pocket, as she was the most tyrannous of autocrats when the reverse was the case.

"Class is dead since the War," she said. "It's all alike these days."

"Never," grunted the old man, deep-rooted in his Toryism. "And never will be in this world — and ope not in the next."

His wife, however, was as dogged as she was dour.

"See Will 'll have Gallops some day," she told the girl one morning with a secret leer over the wash-tub, dropping her voice in a way that would have amused her confidante if it had not offended her.

Esther, sensitive as the elder woman was

coarse, shut up like a flower at the touch of East wind. She came no more to the kitchen of evenings, much as she loved a gossip with the old man over his pipe after the day's work, but spent her off-time in the stable or with the other two land-girls in the cottage where they dossed.

Mrs. Lord's indiscretion made no difference to the girl's relations with the unconscious Will. She knew him too well. Young Will was thinking of marrying as little as she was. Esther was aware of his affair with Milly too: for he had told her.

"That's her," he said, nudging her in the ribs with his elbow, one day as they drove into Barnston in the dray and passed a young woman in the street. "And that's him along of her, I reckon — fine big chap too!" He showed himself mildly interested. "I was glad to be shut on her." He fired his phrases in brief volleys, a long pause between each.

"Ower long i' t' leg and slack i' t' loins to shove int' her collar and keep on at it, I reckon."

That was all he said on the subject; but it was enough.

Esther knew where his heart was. It was as always with his horses, and above all with Boxer and Beauty. Boxer indeed it was clear to the girl had become a passion with him. In her clear-eyed way she saw as plainly as did Lord Gord and his wife that Will was morbid about the horse.

That was where Will's weakness came in. His affections, deep and quiet as an inland sea, were always overcoming him.

CHAPTER TWELVE

On the Road

Late into the autumn Young Will was still working the pair in the plough, and that though they were five off now, full-grown, and broken even to the cart. Esther wondered. She knew that it was the custom to put vanners through their last course at the age of five and take them on the road.

"Oughter move em on," said Mrs. Lord to her with a certain ominous significance. A cruel flicker about her lips and eyes did not escape the girl. Because of it she repeated the remark to Will.

"There's time yet, I reckon," he had replied almost roughly; and it was clear to Esther that breaking the horses to the road was the symbol of some lurking danger that Will dreaded.

She was plodding home through the Croft one misty November evening with the head-horseman, Boxer and Beauty clanking along beside them, after a long day on Sour Pieces, when she was aware of Old William waiting for them in the gate of the yard. She marked on his face the heavy surly look that meant a decision come to and not to be departed from.

"Yo've learnt em the land nigh enough, Will, I'm thinkin," he croaked. "Time yo learnt em the road now."

"They ain't shod behind yet," muttered the head-horseman.

"Then get em shod!" The bulky old man snapped out the words with the snarl that meant he would not be denied. "Take em to farrier to-morrow." He rolled away, saying over his shoulder as he went, "That Box' is funny about his feet. Sure to make trouble. Best take Job along."

"What'd I want wi Job when I got *her*," retorted Will, and jerked in the direction of his lad.

She heard him breathing hard in the dusk of the stable as he slipped Boxer's bridle and put on his head-stall, and was aware that a darkness had descended on his spirit.

As they crossed the yard together he spoke.

"When they're road-trained he'll sell em," he said. "That's where it is."

Next day they led the pair down to the smithy in the village. There was no gainsaying

Old William when he spoke that gait: Young Will and Esther knew that very well. In fact the old man met them as they came back along the lane. It was characteristic of him that he had been watching to see his orders were carried out.

Esther was leading Boxer.

"Well," said the old man, "any fooss?"

"Fooss? . . . Nay," replied Will sullenly. "Never any fooss wi her, I tell thee."

"Then she's the only one there never is any fooss wi — only yo," muttered the old man.

"See dad doesna like Box'," the head-horseman confided to his lad as they tied up. "As lief get shut o him he would. Sell him away into the towns."

She could not see his face, but there was no need. His voice told her all. The bitterness lay for him, she recognized from the inflection in those last words — *into the towns*. She had heard him use that phrase before and always with the same ominous note.

To Will's pure spirit of a child it was clear that the towns denoted something sinister. He was afraid of them. Was it the fear that arises out of ignorance, Esther found herself asking, or out of experience? At least it was obvious that to Will the towns stood as obscene ogres, dark and terrible, crouched away in the mist, the devourers of all children who came within clutch claw of their privy paws.

But Will if he obeyed his father when that worthy set down his foot showed himself to the girl's amusement a master of dilatory tactics when the old man slept, as he did not seldom now.

Somehow or other, on this excuse or that, Will kept his darlings on the land all through that winter. And it was not such an arduous task as you might think when there was much everywhere to be done and few to do it.

It was not in fact till the spring of 1918 that Boxer and Beauty undertook the final course that completes a vanner's education.

They were put in a dray, a train-horse* in the lead, Boxer centre-horse, and Beauty as always in the shafts. Then the head-horseman and his lad led them out to see the world, down the lane, through the village-street on to the King's Highway. They took to the road as ducklings take to water. Hooting motors, rumbling lorries, boys on bicycles, despatch-riders tearing by on eruptive motor-bikes, even traction-engines — nothing disturbed the sedateness of the worldly-wise young pair.

Young Will's pride in their first performance

* A steady old teamster used for training the young.

overcame even his habitual caution. He was for once excited and showed it.

"Might ha been born to it," he reported. "Never looked at nothing — did they, Miss?"

"They just sat down to it," Esther replied, deep-voiced and solemn.

There was only one trouble, and that was quickly rectified. Boxer, always ambitious, was never entirely happy except in the lead. Once he was put there with the train-horse — old Esmeralda it was in this case — between him and Beauty he settled down at once, and more than justified the confidence reposed in him.

"Like a lot more, is young Box'," said Will, with a wink at his lad. "Canna take second place, Box' canna." He was obviously proud of his protégé's pride.

All that summer Boxer and Beauty were on the road making good. That back-end, about Armistice-time, so steady had they proved that Will was using them as train-horses. It was work for which they were admirably fitted. The youngster to be trained was placed between them, centre-horse in the team. If he did not pull his weight Beauty bit him; if on the other hand he rushed Boxer kicked him. In such circumstances, you may be sure, his education proceeded rapidly.

"They're worth pretty nigh their places to

Gallops as train-horses alone," Young Will was careful to say to his lad in his father's hearing.

"Yes, they're coomin on nice now," was all Old William answered as he lumbered away, slobbering his sweet; but Esther caught in his eye the glitter, mischievous and malignant, that meant trouble.

That winter Boxer grew to know every stopping-place upon the road. There was first the turn down to the goods station in the village. If that was passed without the order *Arve! Coom back!* he marched on to the mill. Here he slackened his pull again, and his ears were alert for the steadying *Gee Woa!* When it did not come he surged into his collar and knew his destination was either the market in Barnston or the colliery beyond.

Boxer marched always with the stately tread of a young Emperor, looking about him, expecting and in fact receiving obeisance and admiration from passers-by. He set down his great feet with a peculiar massive delicacy, moving with a slow-swinging rhythm of his body and quarters that made music in the heart of all beholders, pulling so easily, steady as the tide, and as resistless. And he was as amusingly proud and independent as a baby boy who takes his first few steps without his mother. It was clear that he liked to walk alone, self-conducting and majestic. Indeed he

81

showed resentment if even Will went to his head when on the march; while if anybody else attempted it he looked on it as an affront and behaved accordingly.

Young Will soon reached the goal of every self-respecting horse-man with his new team. He drove them without whip or reins, his voice the only guide. That deep-murmured *Gee back!* or *Whoop steady!* of his acted on the leader as surely as the touch of the skilled chauffeur's hand on the steering wheel of a car. At Barnston on market-days, the folk would turn out and stand in their doors, to watch the Gallops "first team" come down the street as they often did for to them fell most of the heavy dray-work in that winter of tumults arising from the War.

Esther did not wonder that Will loved his Boxer. But she was aware that at his heart was the ever-present ache of the young mother who knows that her splendid son will shortly be snatched away from her to school, and the greater his promise and precocity the sooner will the parting come.

He unburthened his heart to the girl one day, as she had always known he would, while they were riding home at evening from Barnston in the empty dray, sitting on the rails in opposite corners, the lights of Gallops twinkling before them.

It was always, Esther noticed, as they turned off the road into the lane at Hangman's Corner that the darkness descended upon Will.

"Yo think we're rough wi em on the land, Miss." *Them* always referred to his horses. "So we are. Got to be if Gallops is to goo on." She had a feeling that he had been waiting for the dusk to cover him before he spoke. "But we aren't cruel like folks in the towns." Those ominous words were always cropping up now in Will's speech with their fatal suggestion of the Doom that knows no mercy and no hope. And the towns, Esther knew, meant for him not the little market-towns such as that they had left an hour since, with their languid buzz of bees droning about their work, but the great cities, such as Sheffield, with greasy cobble-stoned streets, murky with soot and crime, choked with men with ravenous faces, clanging with trams and lorries.

"Men go dark inside of *them* — and I don't blame em," came the quiet voice out of the dusk. "*Gee, Box'. Whoop, Beaut'!* All mucked up together. They grows up crooked — of course they doos. So'd you and me. There's no light and no room. *Arve, Box'! Garn! Coom oop!* It's all dark — in a cellar like — not like here." He swept his hand over the slumbering fields. "In the towns I reckon they should have nowt but motors and machinery and such to do the work. No hörses. If they gets a difficult hörse in there no sayin what they mightn't be up to. See they got him in their power like."

She understood. Will feared what might befall his proud and beautiful Boxer once strange men had him caged in the dark places of the towns, just as of old men feared what would befall their lovely daughters who had been sold into slavery by tyrants.

"Dad don't think o that," came the gentle voice across the dray. "But he's like a son to me, Box' is. Beaut' might be all right. Tain't her. It's ma Box'."

Old William was as always hanging about with a lantern in the yard to watch the team come home. He flashed the beam on to Boxer waiting in the yard to be unhooked and held it there a moment.

"Yes. He's makin into mooney," he said with a purr of satisfaction and the covetous twinkle Esther knew so well.

He too was proud of the first team, as well as he might be. But his love was not pure as was Will's. There was lust in it — the lust of gold.

CHAPTER THIRTEEN

Old William

That winter the Gallops' drays, formed up in line, in the yard, before going into Barnston, made a sight such as our children will never see. There were four of them, each with its three-horse team, and laden to the brim with grain. Boxer led them, as lead-horse of the head-horseman's team; and he knew it. So much his bearing, proud yet sedate, of the King on his way to open Parliament, revealed.

Young Will's heart glowed within him as he walked down the line to take his place at the head.

"Quite a convoy," he would grin in the ear of his lad.

It was always so with him. When the teams were outward-bound he was happy, full of the deep joy and thankfulness of a quiet river running through cattle-dotted summer meads: as they returned home at evening the darkness descended gradually upon his spirit, and the fears got hold of him. And he had cause for fear, seeing that horses of the vanner type were fetching fabulous prices that first winter after the War. Will knew it; and so did his father.

It can hardly have surprised him therefore when the blow fell.

One morning in Barnston, opposite the *Green Man*, when Boxer was just stepping it to take the incline to the market-place with a well-timed rush, a man with a scarf tied about his neck, came out of the bar-parlour into the road.

"What's Mr. Lord want for that bay orse?" he asked harshly.

Will, whip on shoulder, passed him at the double to keep pace with his springing team.

"Sell em together if at all," he answered.

"What! the team?"

"Nay: the pair o bays — lead-hörse, wheel-hörse." Will was well away now, and holding hard to Beauty's head as they raced the hill.

"Tell him I'll gie him three hundred the pair!" shouted the man, glad to let the splendour of his offer resound through the little town.

"They're worth ever penny o four," Will called back.

"Yo'll mind gie dad ma message, Will?"

"Ah," muttered Will.

He did not give it. Esther knew it, and was unhappy because of her knowledge; for she was certain discovery must follow, and with it retribution.

It did, and swiftly. A week passed. Then the dealer came up to Gallops. Esther marked him going into the parlour, a short thick-set swaggering figure. An hour later he came out unaccompanied. When Old William at last emerged, his face was heavy as a mill-stone and as pitiless. Esther saw it and guessed what it foretold. The old man knew Will had deceived him and in so doing betrayed Gallops. It was the unpardonable sin.

"Send Will to me, Missie, wilta?' he said; and she was surprised at his gentleness.

Will went.

The old man was gentle with his son too — terribly so.

"I've sold that bay geldin for £180 to Widgeon," he said hoarsely.

Will, the mildest of men, took fire suddenly. Esther thought the flame of him would have devoured his father. Instead it flickered a moment in the still noon and seemed to die down.

"Yo might ha sold em together, dad," he said quietly. "Make company for em like it so be they got to goo."

For all his quiet she saw that he was quivering.

"Nay." The old man was still as his son was moved. "He's no good to Gallops, isna Box'. Too funnified i the temper. The mare now! She's a nice bit o stuff and kind. I'll use her through hay and harvest and sell her next back-end."

"Then yo'll break her heart — same as yo've broke mine," gulped Will and stumbled off.

The old man showed himself utterly unmoved. Smacking his lips loudly, as he sucked a bull's eye, he lumbered away. It was clear he enjoyed his cruelty; he was so deliberate about it.

Later in the day he met Esther. There was the same heavy almost sullen look about his face, and he threw a swift sly glance at the girl as he passed.

"See Will deceived me. That's why," he mumbled in self-justification.

"Then I think you should tell him so, straight out, Mr. Lord," flashed the girl roused for once by his cruelty out of her habitual calm.

He stopped and blinked at his feet.

"Happen I will," he said.

He did; and Will replied quietly, just as he had done in the morning.

"Yo might ha sold me along o him, dad."

The old man, expecting perhaps violence,

seemed taken a-back by his son's devastating quiet.

"There! there! don't talk silly talk," he muttered and turned away.

". . . For all the use I'm like to be to Gallops without him," continued Will in the same still voice.

That shot went home. Old William paused, half-turned, and cast a suspicious glance at his son out of the corner of his eye. Then he stumped on his way.

"Just is Just," he panted. "Your own doin."

In his heart of hearts there was nothing the old man enjoyed more than playing Jehovah, the Avenger, whose duty and pleasure it is to repay.

Will's distress was terrible. He would not go to the farm. All the evening he sat in Boxer's manger, pulling the horse's ears. Esther, almost as miserable, sat on a truss near by.

"As lief a'most shoot him!" was all he said. "Same as ma young Bounce on the Sommie."

He did not do that: he did something worse.

That night he dealt his father a blow that shook Gallops to its foundations, astounded Birkby Whin, and reverberated even among the pothouses of Barnston.

Esther heard of it first thing next morning. As she was crossing the yard Mrs. Lord rushed out at her, her wisps of gray hair awry. For once the sour woman was flurried, even aghast.

"Will's give his father notice. He's going to Australia."

Esther was shocked: for she knew what that meant.

It meant that Gallops would go.

The blow had staggered even Old William, it seemed. It had been delivered last thing last night as the farmer sat unbuttoned in the kitchen. So tremendous was it, so unexpected, that it was some time before he could realize the full force of it.

Lord Gord had sat blinking before the fire, saying nothing. The shock seemed to have jolted all the life out of him like a punch in the wind. At last he had lugged out the old familiar argument but with an utter lack of the familiar vehemence.

"Gallops got to goo on, I suppose," he had said, feeble and shaking.

"There's Ern," Young Will had answered complacently.

He could be cruel too, astonishingly so, when his heart was touched: for if Ern lasted out the week it would be a miracle.

The old man had risen, unbuttoned as he was, looked at his son with resentful eyes, and had rolled away silently to bed.

Next morning for the first time in history he did not get up.

That action marked as nothing else could have done the portentous nature of the crisis that had arisen at Gallops.

Old William might stay in bed, but he didn't mean to budge in the matter of Box': he had been master of Gallops too long for that. And Will wouldn't budge either.

"No use for Box' no use for me," was all he said, and he said it over and over again.

His mother was in terrible distress.

"I humbled to him and begged him to take it back," the proud woman told the girl.

" '*Box*' was just all he replied."

" '*Dad won't give way*,' I told him."

" '*Nor won't Will*,' he answers, jeery-like."

The hard woman, in tears as she told, begged Esther to speak to Will.

"You're the only one he might give ear to."

Esther was willing to do her best. In her view Will was going altogether too far; and she told him so.

He was sullenly inexorable.

"If Box' goos, I goos."

That was all he would say; and he reiterated his statement endlessly, with the dogged stupidity of a repeating machine.

There was nothing more to be said or done. The situation was a complete impasse that only a miracle could dissolve. Happily the miracle came to pass. The dealer, who had bought Boxer, but had not paid for him, died suddenly of influenza.

CHAPTER FOURTEEN

Boxer Neighs

Gallops breathed again. But the relief was momentary only — everybody knew it: the tension was still there — everybody felt it. Those terrific blows, given and received by father and son, had left their mark, indelible. Sooner or later the clash must recur. And what would happen then? Lord Gord would certainly not give way. Would Will? — Esther was positive he would not, in a matter where Boxer was concerned.

Happily just then salvation came in the invidious form the dealer's sudden death had heralded. The devil of War exorcised at last from earth, another leapt to take its place in the emptied tenement. The winter after the Armistice influenza fell like a flail upon the land. Strong men, who had lived through four years trench-warfare on the West Front, survived the Gallipoli landing, and the desert campaigns, came home at last to die between blankets in comfortable beds, their women and children about them, without making any serious fight at all. It seemed almost as if the life in them had been exhausted in overthrowing the enemy of their country, and there was nothing left to resist the traitor within the gates.

The blast of the new terror smote Gallops like a wind of Death, bringing on its dread wings wrath and destruction.

Old William and his son had to put aside their quarrel and labour shoulder to shoulder to meet the common foeman. There was no time for recriminations, for sulking, for anything indeed but work, work. Gallops had to be kept going, and the stock tended and fed somehow.

"*They* doosn't die, whatever *us* doos," Will commented to his lad with characteristic shrewdness.

The remark was unhappily only too well justified. The head cattle-man went out in forty-eight hours; the third horse-man followed; and the shepherd's wife. Esther was the only one of the land-girls left on her feet. At one time the effective strength of the garrison, twenty or so at normal times, was reduced to Old

William and his wife, Young Will and Esther, a superannuated labourer and a couple of lads.

And how that skeleton crew worked! — perhaps with all the greater zest because some of them at least recognized that the catastrophe was heaven-sent.

Young Will plunged into the battle like a lion. Night and day he laboured as though to prove to his father what his worth to Gallops was. So did Boxer. The work of man and horse was so conspicuous that even Lord Gord was forced to notice it. He showed signs of relenting and made faint gestures towards his son. They were not accepted, to Esther's grief; and the girl realized that the darkness which she had hoped was passing still hung like a pall over Will's fine spirit. He was in no mood for compromise. Concessions, however surprising, would not satisfy him. He would have total surrender or nothing.

In those days Esther noted that he never spoke, except rarely to her and Box'. And she marked a glitter in his eye, of wont so kind, that she did not like. There was in it something despairing, fanatical.

There were others too who marked that strange gleam. At that time even his mother became afraid of Will. Everybody, indeed, except Esther and the old man felt and feared his brooding darkness. And Esther became afraid the evening Will said to her, apropos of nothing, as pitchfork in hand he was mucking out Boxer's stall,

"One thing I know, if dad's took Box' don't ever leave Gallops." He glanced at her; and the girl noted with horror that in his eye there lurked a twinkle of dreadful humour, almost maniacal in its character.

But it was not the old man who was taken.

A morning or two after that remark Lord Gord came to the girl in the stable, where she had been working single-handed: for Will, who since the trouble had done everything himself for his darling, fed, groomed, and harnessed him, had not turned up, to her uneasy surprise.

"Will's down now," said the old man, obviously troubled. "Where's Beaut'?" looking round him. "I got to send a cart into the station for the cake. Must get it oop soom gait." An invoice was in his hand.

Beauty had already gone out in the manure-cart. Two horses had been sent down to be shod. A team had gone into Barnston; and all spare horses had been turned out to take their luck during the shortage of hands.

At the moment there was only one fit horse available, and that horse was Boxer.

"I'll take Boxer," Esther volunteered doubtfully.

She had never driven him even when Will was at her side. Nobody at Gallops had. Will was far too jealous of his prerogative, where his favourite was concerned, to allow another to handle the lines.

The old man moved to the stable-door.

"Never," he said, glum and reluctant, and looked round the yard.

There was nobody about but one ancient labourer, crippled with rheumatism, mucking about feebly with a fork.

"Where's Job?" he asked the girl.

Job was the second horse-man.

"He hung about for Will a bit," Esther answered. "Then he made sure the cake would have come and another horse be wanted; so he's gone up to Skimpots with a sieve of corn and a halter to see if he can catch young Benjamin."

"He canna," snapped the old man. "He's not Will, Job isna."

"I know that then," muttered the girl.

"Why couldna Job take Boxer?" asked Old William suddenly.

Esther hesitated. Then she saw there was nothing for it but to make a clean breast.

"He daren't," she replied briefly. "See since the trouble with Ned Will's forbidden anybody to take Boxer out but himself."

97

Lord Gord turned on her the glare of a baffled bull. He began to shout.

"That's it, is it? Will's forbid *ma* man to take *ma* horse out o *ma* stable. And Gallops may goo down sooner than he should be gainsaid. A'm nowt, A am. And A thowt A was William Lord o Gallops."

He rolled back into the stable and eyed Boxer darkly, chewing his lips.

The great horse from his restlessness, his backward glances, his tuggings at his head-stall, seemed aware of the presence of an enemy.

The old man cast a furtive glance at Esther.

Then he took the bridle off the peg.

"I don't know as I ought to let yo," he mumbled; but after all the law of his being could not be violated and Gallops must go on. So he lent a hand as the girl put the horse in; then he opened the gate of the yard for her, and watched the start.

Boxer was restive going, and worse coming back. Esther was at his head, fighting him all through the village-street. There was nobody about except children: blind windows, shut doors, grey-flint walls that dropped sheer on to the street. As she passed the smithy she realized that she was being gradually over-powered and called out for help; but the noise of the hammers on the anvil drowned her cry. Her hat was off now, and her arm growing tired; but she held on. Boxer's ears were forward. He was tearing away for home, for Will. His rapid walk became a jog-trot. Esther hung on desperately. He tossed her about as he snatched for liberty. They were nearing Hangman's Corner of ominous repute where the lane turned off the highway for the farm. In a moment he would be off at a lumbering gallop. He would be smashed, the cart smashed, she herself smashed.

The girl sobbed as she fought.

Then in front of her she heard a shout. Feet were running, close at hand.

Job, the second horse-man, sent by Old William shot out of the lane.

"All right, Miss!" he called, and leapt at Boxer's head.

Man and girl mastered the horse at length after a terrific conflict by brutal violence.

When it was over and Boxer stood beaten, Esther panting against the shaft, the man looked at her with apologetic eyes, half humourous.

"Nowt for it only that," he said. "Twere him or us."

"I know," gasped Esther.

The man got the cart under way again.

"As well Young Will werena here," he said with a grin.

"Yes," said Esther. "It can't be helped." She

99

felt like a sailor who has been tossed about between decks in a gale. She felt also that she had failed Will and been unworthy of his trust in her.

In the yard Old William was waiting them. He saw at once there had been trouble. Esther was pale, dishevelled, while Boxer stood shifting his feet, seething, blowing his nose.

"Lucky I sent thee along, Job," muttered the old man.

"It *were* that," answered the other. "She'd ha been done else."

Old William regarded the uneasy horse malevolently.

"He's a rough un," he said.

"Yo're right," the man replied. "Cower'd him down under proper we did. Twere the only way. Weren't it, Miss?"

"Yes," said Esther curtly, the shame of her failure still possessing her. She unharnessed the horse herself and led him back to the stall.

He was cowed for the moment as the second horse-man had said. Beauty was back in her place and demonstrated her satisfaction at the return of her mate.

But it was not Beauty for whom Boxer was fretting. Her indeed he ignored. Again and again he broke out into a sweat, do for him what Esther might. He snatched at his head-

100

stall: he stood at attention with alert ears and uneasy feet: he would not rest.

All day he stood thus expectant, waiting, listening; and he would not touch his food. The girl went out and gathered young dandelions to mix with his corn and tempt him, as she had often seen Will do for an ailing horse; but it was of no avail.

Towards evening Boxer threw up his head and neighed.

Esther and the second horse-man watched him.

"It's Will he wants," muttered the man. "He may want too from all I hears."

CHAPTER FIFTEEN

Young Will

Next day it looked as if what the second horse-man had said was coming true. Will was delirious, with rare gleams of consciousness.

On the third day after the doctor's visit it was clear that Will was going.

Everybody at Gallops knew it, especially Box'. He stood in his stall, in a frenzy, whinnying for his friend. And Beauty, distressed because of her mate's distress, put her muzzle above the partition and whinnied too. Those familiar sounds must have streaked with pain Will's tangled dreams as he lay in the little room at the gable-end abutting on the stables, panting out his life.

All that day the men came stealthily one by one, whenever they entered the yard, and peered at the restive horse from the stable-door, only to retire quietly with shaking heads and muttered comment, and return again later on the least excuse, drawn as by a magnet. This mysterious and intimate communion between the great horse, distraught and in travail before their eyes, and the man dying in the gable-end, exercised on them a morbid fascination. And of the two, it was clear from the fragments of their fugitive conversation that it was on Boxer rather than on Will that their interest centred. It was the uncanny quality of the horse's sympathy that held and awed them.

"Never did see the like o yon," in hushed tones.

"And never will."

"It's not in natur."

"Box' is different from the rest. Always was."

"Aye, summat more than just hörse, Box' be."

To his reputation of dangerous was now added the aura of the supernatural.

For two days Boxer did not touch his food. Esther crushed his corn, tempted him with sliced carrots, sprinkled his water with bran. He plunged his muzzle in and out of the bucket and went back to his shrill calling.

The second horse-man stood in the gangway and watched the girl's vain efforts.

"He'll be the next to go, Box' will," he said.

Once Old William came to the door and looked and listened. He said nothing.

That afternoon in one of his passing gleams of consciousness Will sent for his father. The old man went. Not even Martha Lord ever knew precisely what passed between father and son at that last interview.

After it Lord Gord came down into the kitchen, shaking his head.

Martha put down her pans.

"What did he want, dad?"

The old man wandered miserably out.

"If he goos it's all Box' got to goo wi' him — Red Indian style . . . Can't be done. Tain't in reason." He was almost whining.

"Throwin good money in t' dyke. Where'd Gallops be if such like notions held sway?"

That evening as Esther was crossing the yard with a bucket, she was aware of a tapping on the upper floor of the farm.

She looked up. Will was standing at the window of his room in his pyjamas; and there was death in his face.

Desperately he fumbled at the catch, and at length opened it on the bright and bitter March evening. He was delirious clearly, and in his eyes, terrible with confusion and flurried despair, there was a gleam of crazy hope.

"Go back to bed, Will — *do!*" the girl implored.

For all answer he leaned out bare-breasted into the East wind, and handed her stealthily a toy-gun, the treasured relic of his childhood.

"Yo're the only one, Miss," he whispered. "That'll *kill*, but it willna *hurt*. Don't be afraid. Just here, sitha!" He tapped his forehead. "Better that than the towns."

She took the gun to quiet him.

"Box' is all right, Will," the girl told him gently. "You leave all that to me. *Do* go back to bed!"

At that moment Boxer, as if he saw and understood, uttered one of those piercing whinnies of his, short, shrill, desolate.

The man at the window pulled himself together like a mother who calms herself to save her child in the crisis of its illness. His face became kind, his eyes clear. There was a splendour that was visible about his self-denying effort.

"That's ma Box'!" he called in soothing tones. "Woa, ma Boxie-Boy! A'm a-coomin."

That night Young Will died, his hands to his ears, to keep out the sound of Boxer's forlorn crying. It was some hours before the look of desperate resentment and dark conflict on his face passed, to be replaced by an ineffable calm that no winds of the world would ever again ruffle.

When Esther saw the still kind face so familiar to her, she knew that Young Will was himself again, and something more. His sensitive spirit had discovered the secret that placed it at last above pain. He was impregnable, inaccessible, free to love his children and be loved by them without let or hindrance so long as Love abides.

CHAPTER SIXTEEN

The Last Load

Young Will was buried as the Lords of Gallops have been buried time out of mind. No glass-hearse with funeral horses and nodding plumes took him to his grave. The great dray was prepared, washed, greased, painted, and lined with moss according to precedent.

It is the tradition at Gallops that when a horse-man dies his own team takes him his last ride.

Old William would hear of no departure from the rule.

"Gallops style," he said inexorably.

The sentimentalist in him was roused and dogged. Perhaps in the dim deeps of his mind he hoped that by his action he would somehow propitiate Will and whatever gods there be, and make up for past harshness.

And opinion in the yard was with him. Will

had been as well-liked by the hands as a foreman ever is; and it was admitted that this
would have been his wish.

Thus Box' and Beaut' was the order; and Box'
and Beaut' it had to be.

The trouble of course was Boxer. For days
now he had been distraught; and nobody
dared to take him out of the stable. That desolate neighing of his had died down only from
sheer weakness. He would let no one near him
in his stall but Esther. And everyone recognized that the success of the adventure, for
adventure it was, depended solely on the girl.
Martha Lord was obviously worried. She and
the second horse-man had secret interviews. It
was clear to Esther that she had acquired a
momentary and fictitious importance in the
eyes of the community.

"Think we can manage it, Miss?" Job asked
her tentatively.

"We must try," the girl replied.

When the day came she harnessed the horse
and led him out herself, keeping the halter on
under his head-stall.

Boxer, shivering with excitement, made a
rush for the door. Happily the girl squeezed
through first, just escaping being crushed by
his great bulk in the doorway.

He came forging out into the yard. It was a
glorious morning of March, cold and keen. The

sudden plunge into the light that fell all about the horse, clothing him like refreshing raiment, seemed to thrill yet steady him. He stood quite still, a magnificent picture, with high head, alert ears, open nostrils savouring the morning. He was looking about him, looking for Will; and there was tumult in his mind.

The second horse-man led Beauty out and put her in the shafts. Her excitement was referred only from Boxer, who stood quivering like a girl looking for her dilatory lover at a ball. Boxer was hooked in. He was impatient to be on the road, but he was not out of control. It was clear to the girl that he was alive with hope: Will would be in front, in Barnston, waiting.

Esther went to his head: so did the second horse-man. The only chance was to hold him.

He leapt into his collar. The load was light, how light! He stepped eagerly, shaking his head, his ears and eyes everywhere; but he kept within himself.

Down the familiar village-street he paced proudly; on one side the low grey houses on the other the elms in the hedge-row, the pond, the wet field, the purple hedges shimmering with rain-drops. Women and children stood now in the doors, silent all, weeping some. They had been fond of Will.

The dray stopped where it had never

stopped before — at the church upon the mound. Boxer began to fret. He wanted to be moving on to Barnston, to the mill, or the market, where Will would be — if he was anywhere. Esther made much of him, talking to him in her deep voice.

They lifted the coffin out, carried it up the path, and disappeared through the door. Just as the polished brass-handles vanished Boxer neighed frantically. Then he backed, dashed into his collar with a violence almost to snap the chains, scraped with one great foot, and suddenly did what Esther had never known him do before — reared erect.

For a moment he stood there towering, like some heraldic sign, pawing the air, a great ungainly figure, balancing clumsily on uncertain hind-feet. It was touch and go whether he came back on Beauty, much disturbed in the shafts.

Esther leapt at his head: so did the second horse-man. Together they pulled him down.

Old William who had been watching uneasily from the porch of the church came shuffling back down the path and leaned over the wall.

"Take him home afore worse comes of it," he ordered hoarsely. He was surging with anger, darkly suppressed only because of the occasion.

Boxer was plunging hugely now, and Beauty

in a ferment. In another moment they might break away.

"Unhook him!" called Esther sharply.

It was undignified, but it was the only thing to do.

The second horse-man at some risk jumped in and unhooked the leader, while Esther fought at his tossing head. Together they raced him round and made him fast to the tail-board. Once hitched there he was safe.

"Well you brought the halter, Miss," panted Job.

They took the dray home.

Boxer showed himself as eager to rush into his stall as he had been to rush out. What he sought he did not find. Then the heart seemed to die out of him. he stood listless with drooping head and tail. When Esther had unharnessed him he seemed to her smaller, as though some wasting disease was devouring him apace.

She and the second horse-man stood looking at him.

"He's wanin," said Job.

Esther answered nothing. She stayed with the horse, as the dead man would have done. If she could do nothing to allay his troubled spirit at least it might be that her presence in some mysterious sort would comfort him. And she had been Will's best, perhaps his only, human friend. May be Box' knew and appreciated that in the dimness of his submerged consciousness.

Later somebody entered the stable. It was Old William back from the funeral in his baggy blacks and rusty top hat.

He stood in the door-way looking at the horse, and shaking his head, surly and resentful as a baited bear.

"He'll ha to goo," he said. "No good to Gallops, Box' isna."

Esther knew she must make her fight now or never.

"Couldn't you sell them together, Mr. Lord?" she asked — for Will's sake.

Old William moved away, turning in his lips.

"Nay," he said. "I'll keep the mare — for poor Will's sake."

Whether it was cruelty taking covert under its favourite cloak of justice and generosity, finely commingled, Esther never knew. But she knew this: that she was learning daily terrible and illuminating truths about human nature.

CHAPTER SEVENTEEN

Rain

She was in the stable three days later when Old William brought in a man.

Lord Gord's hands were in his pockets, fumbling deep; and on his face the rosy gluttonous look so familiar to Esther. He was pleased with himself: he had made a good bargain. She knew it because he was sucking a peppermint noisily, and rolling it with his tongue, as he invariably did when he had coined money.

His companion looked more like a jockey than a dealer: a dapper little person with tight gaitered legs, very thin, on which he walked delicately, carrying his elbows far from his side. He wore a flat-brimmed hat and smoked a cigar. His face was cadaverous and colourless. The thin skin was stretched tight across the bony framework, and yet for all its tightness there were long creases down the cheeks as if the tissue beneath had wasted away. His eyes were black and there was no light in them; his upper lip enormous and convex. You would say he had never smiled; and that if he did it would be horrible. Esther felt a creeping horror of the man — of both men. Her they ignored.

"That's him," said Lord Gord, nodding at Boxer.

"So I sees," the man answered, sucking the knob of his cutting-whip meditatively.

He leaned up against the post of the stall, sheltering his body behind it. Esther recognized in a flash that this was a customary attitude on his part; thus and thus he would shelter from avenging heels.

Suddenly he drew his cutting-whip and slammed the partition with it viciously.

Boxer leapt, and stood snorting in terror with high head and backward-rolling eyes. How well Esther knew that characteristic attitude of his! How often had she not seen Will go up to soothe his favourite with soft murmurings and gently stroking hands when the great horse's sensitive spirit had taken fright at some imagined peril! The peril, Esther felt deep in her heart, was not imagined now.

The man cackled.

"He's all right," he said.

"Cheap at two 'undud," muttered Old William, sucking loudly.

The two men went to the door and halted there.

"Will you take him now?" asked Old William.

Again the other cackled.

"Nay, I'll send my man to-morrow." He paddled delicately away on his bird-like legs.

It was raining next day when the dealer's man came.

Esther had been waiting for him at Old William's bidding.

He came clod-hopping across the dirty yard, a sodden sack about his shoulders, and hay-bands beneath his knees. He wore huge iron-shod boots in which he walked flat-footed with knees that never bent, and he carried a knobbed and knotted black-thorn. An uncouth Irishman, he had hot red hair and hot red eyes.

"The harse!" he barked. "Come for the harse!"

She led out Boxer into the rain and delivered him over.

He was like a lamb.

The man led him away naked in the rain with downward head and heavy squelching feet that sprayed the mud and water each time they clumped down. Martha Lord was at the

115

window, her ugly face uglier than usual even as she wept.

The men came out of barns and sheds and cow-houses to see the last of Will's favourite. They had never liked Boxer, but they *had* liked Will, and they didn't quite like this.

They gathered in the wet at the gate of the yard, collars about their ears, and watched the big horse slopping away down the lane with streaming quarters and depressed tail.

His quiet surprised and oppressed them. It was unnatural: it was not like the turbulent Box' they knew. Fear overcame them. They stood in a hush of shame like honest men beholding the crucifixion of one they know to be innocent, yet not daring to interfere.

Esther watched them from the stable. She would not join them.

Just then Beauty in her stall whinnied.

There was a movement among the men at the gate. Esther observed their faces, which told her all she could not see herself. There was awe on them, resentment, indignation.

"He's balkin'."

"Yon chap'll learn Box'."

"Box' wants learnin, Box' do," muttered a hind who had both feared the horse and hated him.

"Ah!" A kind of sigh came soughing out of the watchers. "There they goos!"

"Bloody shame!"

Horse and man were fighting already in the rain, and the Irishman was using his bludgeon.

Esther had a smothered glimpse of the scene.

She sickened, went into the stable, and shut the door.

Beauty, her muzzle in the air, was whinnying like a mare for her lost foal.

Her call was answered shrilly from down the lane.

Esther put her hands to her ears . . .

When she removed them at last that long-continued call and the answer, always growing fainter and more desolate, had ceased.

The mare stood alert listening in the silence.

The night that knows no dawn had fallen upon faithful Beauty.